THE GHOST TOWN MYSTERY

created by
GERTRUDE CHANDLER WARNER

Illustrated by Charles Tang

ALBERT WHITMAN & Company
Morton Grove, Illinois

ISBN 0-8075-2859-5

3 5 7 9 10 8 6 4 2

Printed in the U.S.A.

Contents

CHAPTER 1

Tincup Creek or Bust!

Bumpity-bump! Ten-year-old Violet Alden clung to the edge of the Jeep's open window. "This is the bumpiest car we've ever been in," she exclaimed.

"It's the bumpiest *road* we've ever been on," Jessie said, pushing her bangs out of her eyes.

"It's both," agreed Henry, squeezed between his sisters in the backseat. "These four-wheel-drive Jeeps are made to go over rough roads." The oldest at fourteen, Henry knew a lot about automobiles.

Sitting next to Grandfather in the front seat, six-year-old Benny twisted around to talk to his brother and sisters.

"I think it's like a ride at the carnival," he said.

"It's a ride, all right," said Grandfather, laughing. "I forgot my property was located on top of such a high mountain!"

"The Rocky Mountains," Violet said. "They sure are rocky!"

Just that morning the Aldens had left their home in Greenfield, Connecticut. They flew to Denver, Colorado. There Grandfather rented a car at the airport and they drove west into the Rockies. They checked into their motel, Eagles Nest, then set off to find the property Grandfather had recently purchased.

Mrs. Harrington, owner of Eagles Nest, told Grandfather his rental car would never make it up the mountain but her trusty old Jeep would. So Grandfather borrowed the tough little car from her.

Jessie tried to read the survey map, but the fine lines kept blurring. "I hope we're on the right road," she said, concerned.

"Just think if we'd lived in the olden days," commented Grandfather. "Back when there was a gold rush in these parts."

"Gold rush?" Benny asked. "Was that like when we went to Alaska?"

The Aldens had visited Alaska and learned about the gold rush in the Yukon Territory.

"In our nation's history, gold has been discovered more than once," said Grandfather. "The first big gold rush was in California in 1849. Later, gold was found east of here near a mountain called Pikes Peak."

"I read about that," Henry put in. "All these people came out here in covered wagons with banners on the sides that said, 'Pikes Peak or Bust.' "

"We could have come in our boxcar," said Benny. "We would have beaten everybody else."

The others laughed.

When their parents died, the Alden children had no place to live. They found an empty boxcar in the woods that became their home. They knew they had a grandfather, but believed he was mean and hid from him.

Luckily, Grandfather found his grandchildren and took them to live in his big house in Greenfield. Kindhearted James Alden knew the boxcar meant a lot to the children and had it moved to their backyard. The kids never forgot the abandoned train car that kept them together. Now they used it as sort of a clubhouse.

Life with Grandfather was one big adventure, they quickly learned. And now they were beginning a new one.

It started when Grandfather received a call from his old business friend Jay Murphy. Mr. Murphy owned some property in Colorado that he wanted to sell. He offered the land to Grandfather, briefly describing the acreage along Tincup Creek.

Grandfather visited the property when he signed the final papers. When he came back, he was eager to show his grandchildren the land. So he arranged a second trip to Colorado, this time with the children.

James Alden was still chuckling at Benny's idea of traveling west in the red boxcar. "I suppose our banner would say 'Tincup Creek or Bust!'"

"Tincup Creek is one side of our property," reported Jessie. She pressed the map against her knees so the wind wouldn't blow it away.

Violet nodded. "We saw Tincup Creek at Eagles Nest, too."

"The stream is supposed to be great for fishing," Henry said. "I think the guys staying at Eagles Nest are fishermen. At least, they had poles and stuff."

"What a funny name, Tincup," remarked Violet. "I wonder how it got that name." She was trying to glimpse the scenery as the Jeep joggled over a deep rut.

The trees were mostly evergreens, tall and sweet-smelling. Colorful summer wildflowers brushed the sides of the car. Violet had brought her camera, but she'd have to wait until they stopped before she could take any pictures.

Suddenly Grandfather braked hard. They had run out of road.

"Is this it?" asked Benny. "Is this the land you bought?"

Grandfather leaned out of the Jeep's open door. "Not yet. There should be a trail beyond this road. Is that right, Jessie?"

Now she could read the map. "Yes, that's right. The trail doesn't look very long."

"At the end of that trail, the property starts." James Alden grabbed a water bottle in a mesh holder and slung the strap across his shoulder. "Okay, everybody. Let's go!"

Where the rutted, potholed road ended, a narrow trail continued through the trees.

It was a beautiful day for a walk up the mountain. The sun shone brightly in the blue midsummer sky.

"We're at a higher altitude than we were in Connecticut," Henry informed them. "Walking is harder here."

"The altitude doesn't seem to bother Benny," Violet said with a giggle.

"Nothing does," added Jessie. "Except

being late for a meal!" Their younger brother was always hungry.

She was a little hungry herself. Upon their arrival at Eagles Nest, Mrs. Harrington had served them a rather skimpy lunch. From reading the brochure, Jessie knew that Eagles Nest called itself a resort. It was supposed to offer all kinds of activities. The pictures in the glossy pamphlet showed people riding horses and eating delicious-looking meals in the family-style dining room. Eagles Nest even served an afternoon snack.

But when the Aldens had pulled up by the tilted wagon-wheel gate, the run-down cabins didn't look like the ones pictured in the brochure. The three cabins they had reserved weren't ready. Mrs. Harrington's pretty daughter, Marianne, hurried to make up the beds.

Lunch was also late. Instead of the hearty "rancher's" meals the pamphlet promised, they had tuna salad with crackers. There were several cabins, but only two other men were eating in the dining room. Mrs. Harrington had said she was expecting another party later that day.

When Jessie questioned Grandfather about the place, he had replied, "Perhaps Mrs. Harrington has fallen on hard times. Eagles Nest was built back in the fifties. It was probably popular back then. But now it's off the beaten path. Since she became a widow, Mrs. Harrington hasn't kept up the place."

"There aren't any horses or hot-air balloon rides," Jessie had stated, showing him the brochure.

Grandfather shook his head. "Mrs. Harrington told me while you children were unloading the car that she sold the horses years ago. The balloon rides were on another mountain, but that company went out of business, too."

"Well, we're only going to be here a week," Jessie had said. *How bad could it be?* she thought.

Grandfather had nodded in agreement. "With this cool air and these majestic

mountains, we'll feel like pioneers living in those rustic cabins!"

Jessie was pulled out of her thoughts when Benny ran back to her.

"How much farther?" he asked. "It seems like we've been walking *forever*!"

Grandfather wiped his forehead with a handkerchief. "I sure wish my land wasn't on the highest mountain in the Rockies."

"Is it?" asked Violet.

"No," said Grandfather. "I was just joking. But when I was out here earlier, I thought this was the highest mountain!"

Jessie consulted the survey map one last time. "The trail should be ending right about — " She broke off when the path they had been climbing sloped away at their feet.

Everyone stared at the astonishing sight down below, set squarely like a child's blocks.

At the bottom of the canyon were old wooden buildings. Weathered signs were still readable: a barbershop, a dry goods shop, Anderson's Hotel. A wide road split the two rows of buildings.

Grandfather owned a little town!

CHAPTER 2

Grandfather's Town

No one spoke for a moment as they gazed into the canyon. Dust blew down the dirt road that divided the buildings.

"That looks like a Wild West town," said Violet in awe.

"It *is* a Wild West town," Grandfather said with a grin. "And it's ours!"

"You knew about this?" asked Henry.

"I wanted to surprise you," said Grandfather, his grin broadening.

Jessie still couldn't believe it. "Well, you sure did that!" She tapped the map. "How come the town doesn't show up on this map?"

"It's a topological map," Grandfather answered. "It only shows roads and land formations, like mountains and rivers."

"What's the name of our town?" asked Violet.

"Tincup, after the creek," said Grandfather. He checked his watch. "Well, we'd better head back to Eagles Nest for that afternoon snack. We'll have plenty of time to explore the town this week."

Back at the motel, they went into the dining hall, a large room made of logs. Sofas and a fireplace were at one end, while a long table and chairs were arranged at the other.

A lanky young man with carrot-colored hair stood by the fireplace. He stared at Marianne Harrington as she arranged pitchers on the sideboard by the table.

Mrs. Harrington came in when she heard the Aldens enter.

"This is Corey Browne, our new guest," she told James Alden. "He's a student at Colorado State."

"Hey," said the green-eyed young man, still watching Marianne.

Jessie stifled a giggle. It was obvious Corey had a crush on pretty Marianne.

"Ready for snack time?" announced Mrs. Harrington.

"Mmm," said Benny appreciatively. "I'm starving!"

But the "snack" turned out to be a few limp celery and carrot sticks with water to drink. Disappointed, Benny gnawed on a piece of celery.

He was so hungry, he forgot about the town until Grandfather said, "Mrs. Harrington, I showed my grandchildren the town. What do you know about it?"

The motel owner sat down at the table.

"It's quite a story," she began. "Tincup," she said, "is a ghost town!"

For some reason, Violet shivered. "A ghost town! That's neat," she said.

"It's been that way for over a hundred years," said Mrs. Harrington. "Way back, a forty-niner going home camped at Tincup

Creek." Then she explained, "A forty-niner was somebody who went to California for the 1849 gold rush. His name was Duncan Payne. One morning he washed his face in the stream and saw something yellow, like gold."

Everyone at the table became still.

"Duncan had sold his mining stuff before leaving California," said Mrs. Harrington. "All he had was a knife and a tin cup. He dipped the cup in the stream and caught the gold. Duncan dug and dug, but he didn't find much gold. He *did* find a lot of black sand along the creek. He took samples of the sand back to Denver. It turned out to be silver ore."

Corey nodded. "Silver is an important part of Colorado's history. But it's hard to find. No one had ever paid any attention to the black sand along the creeks," he said loudly.

Corey seemed nice, thought Violet, but she didn't like the way he practically yelled when he spoke.

"Until Duncan Payne came along," Mrs. Harrington said. "Duncan started a mine.

Soon a town was built near the mine. It was called Tincup after the gold Duncan found in his tin cup."

"I have a cup," said Benny. "It's old, too. I used to drink milk out of it."

Mrs. Harrington went on with her story. "The town of Tincup grew. Singers and dancers and actors came to entertain the miners. One night during an opera, Duncan fell in love with a singer. Her name was Rose. She had beautiful blue eyes and black hair down to her knees."

Jessie hugged herself with delight. "This is so romantic!"

"Then what happened?" Violet asked eagerly.

Mrs. Harrington smiled. "Duncan and Rose married and built a mansion above Tincup, near the mine. They had a daughter named Seraphina. Seraphina went to eastern schools. They traveled all over Europe. They were rich and happy. And then" — she lowered her voice — "trouble struck."

At that moment, the door to the dining hall opened. Two men came in.

One had sandy hair and gray eyes that crinkled at the corners. His shirt was crisply ironed and his jeans were neat.

The other man was nearly bald and wore glasses. He wore a tattered vest with mesh pockets and fishing hooks poked through loops. He scowled when he saw the others at the table.

Henry wondered why the second stranger seemed so sour when no one had even said anything to him yet. At first Henry thought the two men were together, but they sat at opposite ends of the table.

The first man said, "Adele, do you have any iced tea?"

"Sorry," said Mrs. Harrington. "Just water. Marianne, fetch the gentlemen some water."

Marianne, who had been quietly folding worn napkins, got up to pour the newcomers glasses of water.

"Everybody," announced Mrs. Harrington, "this is Victor Lacey." The sandy-haired man smiled and raised his glass in a friendly way. "And our other guest is Robert

Williams," added Mrs. Harrington.

Robert Williams nodded formally. Now Henry knew the two men had not come to Eagles Nest together. They were so different, they couldn't possibly be friends. Henry also noticed that Victor Lacey called the motel owner by her first name. Mr. Lacey must have been staying here awhile.

"They are here to try their luck at trout fishing," said Mrs. Harrington. She introduced the two men to the Aldens, and told them that the Aldens were visiting to see the land and the town that they owned.

Benny wanted to get back to the story. "What happened to Duncan and Rose?"

"It's so sad," said Mrs. Harrington mournfully. To the newcomers she said, "I'm telling the story of the old town at the bottom of the canyon. You might have seen it."

Mr. Lacey gazed over his glass with round gray eyes. "There's an old town around here?"

"You'll see it if you go hiking," said Grandfather.

"Tincup wasn't the only silver-mining town," Mrs. Harrington went on. "The West was full of them. But too much silver was being used for money. So President Cleveland lied to the silver-mine owners and told them gold would be used for money instead."

"What happened to the silver mines?" asked Jessie.

"They closed," replied Grandfather. "Overnight the mines shut down."

"The miners had to leave," Mrs. Harrington said, taking up the story again. "Soon towns like Tincup were empty. They became ghost towns because no one lived in them."

Now even Corey was interested. "So what became of Duncan and Rose?"

"Duncan was suddenly broke," answered Mrs. Harrington. "The men who abandoned the mines had to start over. Most of them didn't have much money. They built rafts and floated down rivers to big cities to find work. Duncan, who was not a young man, joined a group on a homemade raft.

There was a storm on the Colorado River one night. The raft broke up and he was killed."

The dining room was silent.

"Poor Rose," said Violet. "What did she do?"

Mrs. Harrington leaned forward. "Before he left, Duncan told her he would be back someday and to look for him at sundown. Rose Payne stayed in the mansion above Tincup. Every day she sat in her chair, watching until the sun began to drop over the cliff wall. Then she'd take the trail down to Tincup and walk toward the setting sun."

"What was she doing?" asked Benny.

"Going to meet her husband," Mrs. Harrington said dramatically. "Even after she knew he'd been killed, Rose Payne left her house and walked toward the sunset every single day."

Grandfather had a question. "We didn't see the mansion. Where is it?"

"Gone," said Mrs. Harrington with a wave of her hand. "It was built near the mine on top of the mountain. Rose refused to leave or let anyone fix it. So the mansion fell to pieces around her."

"But the town is still there," said Corey. "Cool!"

"Wow!" exclaimed Victor Lacey. "That's some yarn! What are you going to do with your ghost town, Mr. Alden?"

Grandfather shook his head. "I have no idea."

Benny was excited about the idea of owning a town. "Can I be the police chief?"

Everyone laughed, breaking the spell of Rose and Duncan Payne's tragic story.

The "snack" over, Marianne hustled over to clear away the glasses.

"You've lived near a ghost town all your life," Jessie said to the young woman. "What's it like?"

Marianne bent down. "Mother didn't tell you the *whole* story," she said mysteriously.

"What didn't she tell us?" asked Jessie.

But Marianne whisked away Jessie's glass, saying only, "You'll find out soon enough."

CHAPTER 3

The Lady in Gray

"I wonder what she meant by that?" Violet asked when Jessie told the others about Marianne's strange remark.

"She said we'd find out soon enough," Henry said, glancing around. "Talk about the Payne mansion. *This* place is falling apart. I wonder why Mrs. Harrington doesn't make any repairs."

Jessie stopped in front of the cabin she was sharing with Violet. "Grandfather told me earlier he thinks Mrs. Harrington has fallen on hard times. She probably can't afford to have the repairs made."

Henry unlocked the door to his and Benny's cabin. "I can see why. It's the middle of summer and hardly anybody is staying here."

"We'll see you guys after we've unpacked and cleaned up," Jessie said to the boys. "Then Grandfather is taking us back to see the town."

"I still can't believe we own our very own town!" Benny exclaimed. "I want to be fire chief *and* police chief!"

Violet giggled. "I don't think there are fires or criminals, Benny. Nobody lives there!"

She and Jessie went inside their cabin. The place had been cute once but now was shabby. Faded red-checked curtains hung at the single window. The knotty pine bunks were covered with Indian blankets, the holes darned many times. Dusty pictures of the Rockies hung on the walls.

The girls stowed their clothing in the small dresser, then Jessie decided to take a quick shower.

She came right out of the bathroom. "We have no towels."

"I saw Marianne put some in there before she made up the beds," Violet answered.

"Well, there aren't any now." Jessie went over to the phone on the pine stand between the bunks and picked up the receiver. A frown crossed her face as she jiggled the connector button.

"What's wrong?" asked Violet.

"The phone isn't working," replied Jessie. "We've got to have towels. I'll borrow some from the boys."

But Henry and Benny didn't have towels, either.

"This is weird," said Violet. "I'll go up to the main office and get some."

She came back a few moments later with a stack of threadbare towels. "Mrs. Harrington gave me a funny look. She said all the cabins are supplied with linens."

"Why would we fib about towels?" asked Jessie. "Surely she doesn't think we stole them?" She held up one. "These barely make good rags."

Henry took half of the towels for his and Benny's bathroom. "Eagles Nest is weird, don't you think?"

As Violet waited for Jessie to take her shower, she thought Benny might be right. Eagles Nest *was* odd — and so were the people who ran it. Dead phones, missing towels . . . what would happen next?

"I'll never get used to this road!" Henry yelled as the Jeep tore up the mountain.

The Aldens were glad when the road finally ran out and Grandfather parked the Jeep. Early evening sunlight dappled the trail. Now that they were aware of the altitude, they didn't try to climb so fast.

"What are you going to do with your property?" Henry asked his grandfather.

Grandfather pondered the question. "I really don't know yet. What do you children think I should do with it?"

"Aldenville?" Jessie chuckled.

"No! Bennytown!" If Benny had a town named after himself, he could be mayor, police chief, *and* fire chief.

Before the trail ended at the canyon, where they had first glimpsed the ghost town, another trail branched off, an old unused road. Mrs. Harrington had told the Aldens to take this road down into the canyon.

They found the fork in the path and soon were walking down the dirt road, now overgrown with weeds.

"This is the old wagon road," Grandfather said. "It seems steep and twisty, but a team of horses could get down into the canyon on it."

"I bet that ride would be wilder than in our Jeep!" Benny exclaimed, running ahead.

The road took one more turn, then straightened to become the main street of the ghost town. A wooden sign with faint letters announced the town of Tincup.

Benny waited for the others before entering the town.

"All right," said Grandfather firmly. "No one is to enter any buildings unless I go, too. Remember, these buildings are more than a hundred years old. The flooring could be rotted. Consider them dangerous."

The children nodded. Stores and other buildings lined either side of the street. Many had wooden awnings.

"We'll just stroll down Main Street first," Grandfather went on. "Then we'll explore indoors."

As anxious as Henry had been to reach the old town, he found himself walking cautiously down the dusty road. Signboards flapped in the rising wind. *Creak! Creak!* went the barbershop shingle. Tincup was *creepy*.

Jessie was thinking the same thing. *Not a living soul stays here.* Mrs. Harrington's whispered words came back to her.

Grandfather finally broke the eerie silence. "See the raised sidewalks?" He pointed to the shallow wooden platforms built in front of the stores and the two hotels. "They didn't have concrete back in those days. So they made sidewalks out of wood. Women wouldn't get the hems of their long dresses muddied or dusty."

Violet had also been under the spooky

spell of the empty old place. She was glad to picture real people in Tincup.

"I bet their dresses were really pretty," she said.

Jessie nodded. "But those gowns were hard to move around in. I'd rather wear jeans any day!"

Benny pointed to wooden poles in front of the dry goods shop. "What are those for?" he asked.

"Those are hitching posts," answered Henry. "When a rider came into town on his horse, he looped the reins over the hitching post so his horse wouldn't wander off."

"Like parking a car," Benny said.

Jessie giggled. Benny could always make them laugh. "Yes, the cowboys parked their horses!"

"Can we go into one of the buildings now?" Benny asked Grandfather. "Like that one?" He pointed to the dry goods shop.

"Let me check it out first," Grandfather replied. "I don't want anyone getting hurt."

"You be careful, too," said Violet. She

worried about Grandfather, even though he was healthy and fit.

The children waited as he opened the door, which hung off a broken hinge, and disappeared inside.

The sun was sinking below the rim of the canyon, high above the town. The wind picked up, tumbling twigs and leaves down the deserted street.

Just as the sun touched the edge of the canyon, like a fireball in the sky, Violet noticed something.

A figure was standing at the end of town.

Violet gasped, and the others looked, too.

The figure was clearly a woman, dressed in a long, plain gray dress. Her back was turned to the children. A light gray shawl was wrapped tightly around the woman's shoulders. Stringy gray hair blew in the wind.

"Who is that?" Jessie whispered.

"I don't know," said Henry. "But I think we should tell Grandfather."

Just then the sun sank over the ledge, leaving a purple haze over Tincup.

"Grandfather!" Benny called. "Come quick!"

James Alden hurried through the door. "What is it?"

"There's a lady — " Violet began.

But the woman had vanished.

"What lady?" quizzed Grandfather. "I don't see anybody."

"She was *here*," Jessie insisted. "We all saw her. She had on a long dress."

Grandfather stared at them. "I believe you saw *something*. The altitude can play tricks on your eyes."

"It wasn't a trick," Violet said. "We saw a lady."

"We'd better go back to Eagles Nest," said Grandfather. "Maybe Mrs. Harrington knows about this mysterious lady."

Everyone was silent as they climbed the wagon road and then the trail back to the Jeep.

At Eagles Nest, dinner was about to be served. Mrs. Harrington urged the Aldens to sit down at the large table. Mr. Lacey, Mr. Williams, and Corey were already seated.

"How was your trip into Tincup?" asked Mrs. Harrington.

"My grandchildren saw someone," Grandfather replied. "A woman. By the time I got there, she was gone."

"Was the woman walking toward the sunset?" asked Mrs. Harrington.

"Yes!" answered the Alden children at once.

"But then she disappeared," added Benny.

"Right as the sun went down?" Mrs. Harrington prompted.

"Yeah," said Benny. "How'd you know?"

Mrs. Harrington nodded sagely. "You children saw someone very special."

"Who?" asked Jessie, her spine already tingling.

"Rose Payne."

Grandfather's eyebrows lifted. "Duncan Payne's wife? But Rose Payne is long dead."

"Yes," said Mrs. Harrington. "But the ghost of Rose Payne is still here. Mr. Alden, you bought a ghost town that comes with its very own ghost!"

CHAPTER 4

The Mysterious Letter

"A ghost!" Benny breathed.

"Cool," said Corey in his loud voice. "A real, live ghost in a ghost town. Get it?" he asked Marianne as she poured water into his glass.

The pretty waitress simply ignored him. By now her mother had returned from the kitchen with a large tray. Mrs. Harrington and Marianne began setting plates in front of the diners.

"There's no such thing as ghosts, Benny," Grandfather said. "You know that."

"But we *saw* this lady!" he insisted.

"You children saw a person," Mr. Williams said, speaking for the first time. "It couldn't have been a ghost."

Deep inside, Henry knew his grandfather and Mr. Williams were right. But he, too, had seen the Lady in Gray. She had moved as if she were floating on air. And when they called Grandfather to come out of the dry goods store, she had vanished.

"If the lady was a real person, why didn't she talk to us?" asked Jessie.

Mrs. Harrington nodded in agreement. "The children definitely saw the ghost of Rose Payne. That's what she did during her last years — went down to the town and walked into the sunset. She never stopped waiting for her husband."

"Romantic hogwash!" Mr. Williams said gruffly. "Mrs. Harrington, you're filling these children's heads with a ridiculous story."

"It's not a story!" Mrs. Harrington said, bristling. "I've lived on this mountain nearly all my life. I've seen the ghost of Rose

Payne. I know it's true." She set Mr. Williams's plate in front of him with a thump.

He poked at the sauce-covered lump on his plate. "What is this supposed to be?"

"Fried chicken with gravy," the owner replied. "An old family recipe." Then she and Marianne left to bring out the bread and a pitcher of water.

Victor Lacey stabbed tentatively at his dinner. "If this is chicken, I'll eat my hat."

Benny giggled at the thought of Mr. Lacey chewing his fishing hat. But after tasting the chicken, he gave up on the meat. The rest of dinner was just as awful. Mushy Brussels sprouts, burned rolls, salty mashed potatoes, and limp, watery spinach. It was the worst meal he had ever eaten.

"If there aren't any ghosts, then who did we see?" Violet asked her grandfather.

James Alden shook his head. "I didn't see your lady, so I can't answer that. But we'll visit Tincup more while we're here. Maybe I'll see her, too."

The guests finished their dinners in silence.

"Not too many hearty appetites," Mrs. Harrington remarked as she poured coffee for the men, and Marianne cleared away the dishes. "After a night of sleeping in this fresh country air, you'll be ready for a big rancher's breakfast."

Jessie hoped it would be better than supper.

Marianne brought in dessert.

"Brownies!" Benny exclaimed. "I love brownies." But not these. His was so hard, he couldn't bite into it.

As Marianne took her plate, Jessie asked the young woman, "Do you believe in the ghost?"

Marianne looked around quickly. Several people were staring at her — Corey, Victor Lacey, and her mother. It was as if they were waiting for her answer.

"Yes," Marianne whispered finally. "I do."

Jessie didn't know if she believed Marianne or not. Was the young woman simply saying she did because her mother was watching her? Mrs. Harrington certainly believed in the ghost, or at least she gave that impression.

Corey fiddled nervously with his fork. Then he asked Marianne, "Would you like to go on a walk with me after supper?"

"I can't," Marianne said briskly, not even glancing in his direction. "I have too much work to do."

"How about when you're finished?" Corey pressed. Jessie could tell he really liked the pretty girl.

But Marianne just shook her head and hustled away with the tray of dirty dishes.

Dinner over, the Aldens retired to their cabins. Before settling in for the night, the children met in Henry and Benny's cabin to discuss the day's events.

"I'm still hungry," Benny moaned, sitting on his bunk.

"So am I," Henry agreed. "That dinner was terrible."

Violet nodded. "Mrs. Harrington doesn't seem to be a very good cook. But she's been running Eagles Nest a long time. She *should* be."

"Maybe that's why there aren't very many people staying here," Jessie concluded.

"When people go on vacation, they expect nice, clean rooms and good food."

"Don't talk about food anymore," Benny begged. "It makes my stomach growl. Let's talk about the ghost."

Always the voice of reason, Henry told him gently, "We know ghosts don't really exist."

"But if it wasn't a ghost, then who was it?" Benny demanded.

"I don't know," Henry replied. "But we saw . . . somebody."

"Who? And why was she in Tincup?" asked Violet. "There's absolutely nothing in that town except dust and tumbleweeds."

Benny bunched his flat pillow so he could rest his head. "I like Tincup. I think it's neat."

"It is neat. But there's no way anybody could live there." Violet looked at her older sister. "What did you ask Marianne?"

"I wanted to know if she believed in the ghost," Jessie replied. "Before she answered me, she kind of glanced around to see who was listening."

"Who was listening?" asked Benny.

"Her mother was watching us," Jessie replied. "And Mr. Lacey and Corey."

"Corey likes Marianne," Violet put in. She could see why. Marianne was so beautiful, with her jet-black hair and sky-blue eyes.

"I don't think she likes *him*," Jessie said. "Corey's so loud. And his jokes are bad. But Marianne acted strange when I asked her about the ghost. Like she was afraid."

"What would she have to be afraid of?" Henry wondered.

At that moment, a loud *clang* caused them all to jump.

"What was that!" Benny exclaimed.

"It came from the bathroom." Henry went to investigate. He returned with a U-shaped pipe. "Don't plan on using our sink tonight, Benny."

Jessie recognized the pipe as the part that curved under the sink. She shook her head. "This place is a disaster! You guys can use our sink till Mrs. Harrington gets yours fixed."

"*If* she gets it fixed," Henry said.

*   *   *

The next morning, the boys met Victor Lacey on their way to the dining hall. Benny carried the curved pipe.

"Did that fall out of your sink?" asked Mr. Lacey.

Henry nodded. "We're going to tell Mrs. Harrington to call a plumber."

"I can fix that in a jiffy. All I need is a wrench." He left to fetch Mrs. Harrington's toolbox. Then Mr. Lacey quickly fitted the pipe back under the sink. As he tested the water so it drained properly, he said, "Mrs. H needs a handyman. Repairmen in Beaverton are too far away."

Benny was admiring the tools in the metal box. "I could be her handyman." It sounded like a neat job, along with mayor, police chief, and fire chief of Tincup. Benny liked to be busy.

Henry noted the tools were caked with grease. No one had used them in a long time. Maybe not since Mr. Harrington had died. "Thanks," he told Mr. Lacey. He also wondered how Mr. Lacey knew where to find the toolbox. How long had the man been staying here?

"No problem." The sandy-haired man smiled. "Let's go have that hearty rancher's breakfast!"

"I'm starving!" Benny declared. He hoped there would be stacks of pancakes dripping with maple syrup, crispy bacon, eggs, and buttered toast with strawberry jam.

But when he and the other Aldens sat down at the big table, they saw only bowls of runny oatmeal. The tiny glasses of orange juice had seeds floating in them.

"This is a hearty rancher's breakfast?" Violet whispered to Grandfather, who sat on the other side of her.

Grandfather never complained, but he smiled as he ate the soupy oatmeal. "If I lived on this ranch, I don't know if I'd have enough strength to climb on my horse, much less ride the range!"

The children giggled. Grandfather could always make them laugh.

But Mr. Williams wasn't amused. He

tossed his spoon down in disgust and demanded more coffee.

Victor Lacey ate his cereal gamely. "I have something for you, Mr. Alden," he said. "I hope you don't mind a little business at breakfast."

"Well, it was a *little* breakfast so a *little* business should go along with it just fine," Grandfather joked as he took the envelope Victor handed him across the table.

The children waited anxiously as Grandfather slit the flap and pulled out a single sheet of paper.

James Alden's eyebrows shot upward and he gave a low whistle.

"What is it?" Benny asked.

"Mr. Lacey is offering to buy my property," Grandfather replied. To Victor he said, "This is a very generous offer. Much more than I paid for the land."

Victor shrugged. "Since I've been out here, I've taken a fancy to the place. The land is worthless commercially, but I'd like to have it."

Grandfather put the paper back in its envelope and slipped the envelope into his jacket pocket. "Let me think about it. I'm quite surprised."

After breakfast, the children walked out with Grandfather.

"What was that all about?" Henry asked.

"I'm not sure," said Grandfather.

"What did Mr. Lacey mean when he said the land is worthless?" asked Violet.

"He meant it's not suitable for development," Grandfather replied.

"Like for shopping centers and apartments," Jessie added.

"Not only that, but he offered me a lot of money for it!" Grandfather shook his head in amazement.

"If the land is so worthless," Violet wanted to know, "then why does Victor Lacey want it?"

"Good question," said Grandfather. "Children, I think you have a new mystery to solve!"

CHAPTER 5

"*Get Off My Land!*"

"What are you going to do?" Benny asked Grandfather.

"Well, first I must call Jay Murphy, my friend who sold me the property, and see what he thinks about Mr. Lacey's offer," said Grandfather. "I've only owned the property a few weeks. But Jay had that land for years. He knows more about this area than I do."

"There's a phone in the dining hall," Violet said.

James Alden glanced back at the log

building. "Yes, it's on the small table for the guests' use. However, it's too public. I'll use the phone in my cabin."

The children followed him inside. Grandfather's cabin was as shabby as the others. A broken shade was tacked crookedly at the window. The carpet was stained and ripped.

Grandfather picked up the receiver and jiggled the connector button. "No dial tone," he said, frowning.

"Ours was dead last night," said Jessie. "When I tried to call for towels."

At that moment, Marianne Harrington passed by the open door.

"Miss," Grandfather called. "Our phone is dead."

"They're all dead," Marianne replied. "It happens a lot up here."

"But we didn't have a storm last night," said Henry. "What would cause the phone service to go out?"

Marianne merely shrugged and continued on her way.

"Now what?" Violet said.

Grandfather sighed. "I'll have to drive

into Beaverton. That's the nearest town with a phone."

"Would you buy us some food?" Benny asked. "I'm still hungry from breakfast!"

"I can top that. I'm still hungry from dinner last night," Henry added.

"I'll get some snacks and juices," Grandfather promised.

"Do you want us to come with you?" Jessie asked.

Grandfather smiled. "You children stay here and enjoy this gorgeous day." Then he climbed into his rental car and drove away.

The other guests were off on various pursuits. Victor Lacey and Robert Williams had gone fishing. Corey had strapped on a huge backpack and left on a long hike.

Except for Marianne and Mrs. Harrington, who were busy, the Alden children were alone at Eagles Nest.

"I wish we could take a hike, too," said Violet. "The mountains are so beautiful."

Just then Mrs. Harrington came out of the dining hall with a garbage can. She overheard Violet's remark.

"You can go hiking," the owner suggested. "There's an easy trail just past the last cabin. It's well marked. You'll be perfectly safe."

Excited, the kids changed into hiking boots and shorts. Marianne fixed them paper sack lunches with sandwiches, little bags of potato chips, apples, and bottles of water.

Beyond the last cabin, they found the trail and began the climb uphill.

This time Violet brought her camera. She stopped often to snap pictures of breathtaking views. She kept hoping they'd see an animal, but the wildlife must have heard their clumping boots and stayed hidden.

When they reached a flat spot in the trail, the children sat down to eat.

Benny opened his bag eagerly. Then he stared at his sandwich.

"Peanut butter and *cucumbers*?" he exclaimed in disbelief. "Who ever heard of a peanut-butter-and-cucumber sandwich?"

"You got the good one," Jessie said, peek-

ing between two slices of stale bread. "I have grape jelly and *spinach*. Left over from last night's dinner, I bet."

Henry's and Violet's sandwiches were just as awful. The children made do by pulling out the vegetables and eating the bread. At least the potato chips and apples were okay.

When lunch was over, the children perched on a large boulder and stretched out in the noonday sun.

"Look!" Henry cried. "An eagle!"

Fascinated, they watched the eagle's lazy flight.

"I wish I could fly," Benny said dreamily. The warm sun made him sleepy. He closed his eyes for a second.

Then Jessie was shaking him. "Benny, wake up."

"I'm awake," he said, sitting up. "Where are we?"

"We're still on the mountain, but we should head back to the motel," Violet said as she gathered their trash into one sack.

Henry slid down off the rock and helped the others.

"Here's the trail," he said. But it seemed different. Were those three round rocks there before? he wondered.

At first no one else noticed if the trail looked different.

Then Jessie said, "I don't remember that raggedy mountain peak way off in the distance."

"I don't, either," said Violet. "I took lots of pictures, but not one of that mountain."

"We're going downhill," Benny pointed out. "We must be on the right trail."

But the more they walked, the more Henry realized they were on the wrong trail.

"Stop, guys. We're lost," he admitted. "It's my fault. I should have looked around for a second trail."

"We all should have been paying attention," Jessie said, trying to make him feel better.

Benny climbed onto a fallen tree. "Hey!" he yelled. "I see smoke!"

Henry quickly joined him. "Smoke means a campsite or maybe even a cabin! Let's go down."

They followed the trail to a sunlit clearing. In the center was an old but well-built cabin. Smoke curled from its stone chimney.

"Somebody's home," Violet said excitedly. "I'm sure they'll help us find our way back to Eagles Nest."

Jessie walked up to the solid door and knocked.

At once, the door flung inward and a huge figure filled the doorway.

"What do you want?" a booming voice demanded.

Benny immediately thought of a giant in a fairy tale.

"I — uh — " Jessie stammered. She fell back a step, startled.

The large figure was a woman. She wore a red-and-black flannel shirt over at least two other shirts and men's jeans. Her large feet were laced into stout work boots. The woman's iron-gray hair was cut short and jaggedly, as if she'd cut it herself with scissors and no mirror.

"What do you want?" the woman demanded again.

This time Henry spoke up. "We were hiking and we got on the wrong trail — "

"You sure did!" the woman boomed. "This is private property. Get off my land!"

"But — " Before Henry could finish his sentence, the woman went back into the cabin and slammed the door.

The Aldens stared at one another, astonished by the huge, unfriendly woman.

"We won't find any help here," Henry said. "Let's get off the lady's property like she asked. Maybe we'll find the right trail if we keep looking."

In the end, Benny found a fork in the trail. Soon they were back at Eagles Nest.

"Just in time for afternoon refreshments," Mrs. Harrington told them, setting out a bowl of olives.

Benny didn't like olives with pits. "No, thanks," he said. "But something happened up on the trail!"

"You didn't see a bear, did you?" asked Mrs. Harrington.

"Worse! We saw this lady who was almost as big as a bear!"

Jessie giggled at her brother's description. "We got on the wrong trail and wound up at a cabin. The lady who lived there wasn't very friendly."

"She told us to get off her land," Violet added. "She shut the door in our faces."

Mrs. Harrington nodded. "That was Old Gert you ran into. She's harmless, unless she catches you trespassing."

"Why would a woman want to live in the woods by herself? Doesn't she get lonely?" Jessie asked.

Mrs. Harrington shrugged. "Old Gert's been on that mountain since my Walt brought me here as a bride. She likes to be alone. Just remember she's harmless, but *tough*," she warned. "Don't cross her path."

Violet knew Gert was scary, but there was something familiar about the old woman. Something she couldn't put her finger on.

The kids went outside to wait for Grandfather, who hadn't returned from Beaverton yet.

"Do you think Old Gert could be the ghost?" Jessie suggested. "She doesn't like people around. It would be a good way to scare off people."

Violet shook her head. "She's too big. The Lady in Gray is smaller and thinner." Was that what was bothering her? No, it was something else.

"It was hard to tell how thin Old Gert is, with all those shirts she had on," Henry said. "But I think Violet's right. Gert was too tall to be the ghost."

Just then Grandfather's rental car pulled up. As he climbed out, the children ran over.

"Did you talk to Mr. Murphy?" asked Benny. "What did he say?"

"Yes, I did," Grandfather answered. "Jay reminded me the property had just been assessed."

"What does that mean?" Violet wanted to know.

Henry replied, "It's when someone figures out the value of the land."

Grandfather nodded. "The assessed value is often higher than a buyer's asking price. People want to save some money and everyone expects it. But Victor's offer is a *lot* more than I paid. And way above the assessed value. It doesn't make sense."

Jessie frowned. "Mr. Lacey said your land is worthless. What did Mr. Murphy say about that?"

"Jay didn't know why Mr. Lacey said the land was worthless," Grandfather went on. "There isn't anything wrong with that property. It's just not worth a lot."

But Mr. Lacey wants it, Jessie thought. *Bad enough to pay a whole lot of money.*

That night the lights went out during dinner. The food was so horrible it was just as well they didn't have to look at it, Violet decided.

"We have electricity problems here," Mrs. Harrington said, lighting a single lantern and setting it on the table. "The power truck should come out tonight to fix it."

Mr. Williams tossed his napkin beside his plate. "Mrs. Harrington, if I catch some trout tomorrow, would you cook it for supper?"

Benny's mouth watered at the thought of trout, even though he didn't like fish that much. But anything would be better than the barely warmed frozen pizza they were eating.

"Sure," said Mrs. Harrington. "But don't get your hopes up. Tincup Creek is all fished out."

"How can a stream be fished out?" asked Benny.

Corey explained, "A lot of streams in the West are in danger. There are more people catching fish than fish being born. The streams need to be restocked with trout."

No fish in the stream, falling-down cabins, poor food, electricity and phones that went out for no reason. No wonder Eagles Nest had so few tourists, Henry thought as he and Benny went to their cabin.

"I can't see," said Benny. "It's so dark!"

"Let's open the shade," Henry suggested. "Maybe a little moonlight will shine in."

But clouds covered the moon and stars. Henry and Benny couldn't see anything. But they heard voices arguing.

"It's only for a couple more days," said a shrill voice.

"I don't care! I don't want to!" whispered a lower voice.

Benny put his hand on Henry's arm. "Who's out there?"

"Two women," said his brother. "I think it's Marianne and her mother."

"Or Old Gert," supplied Benny.

"That's possible," Henry said.

Then the one with the shrill voice said, "It's for a good cause!"

"I don't care!" said the whisperer. "I won't do it! I won't!" Sobbing, she ran down the path.

As Benny got ready for bed in the dark, he wondered about the whisperer. What was it she didn't want to do? And who was making her do it?

CHAPTER 6

Vanished!

The next morning, over a breakfast of cold cereal, the children discussed the latest mysterious events.

"The two people arguing must have been Marianne and her mother," Jessie said. "They are the only two women here."

"Don't forget Old Gert," said Benny.

Violet frowned. "But why would Gert argue with one of the Harringtons? She never leaves her mountain."

"I've been thinking," said Henry. "Besides Grandfather, Victor Lacey and Mr.

Williams both have their own rental cars. Maybe they drove into Beaverton and brought someone back with them."

Jessie looked at him. "Are you saying the ghost might be somebody we haven't met at Eagles Nest?"

"It's a possibility," said Henry. "At least the electricity is back on. Did anyone hear a power truck last night?"

No one had. It was so quiet at Eagles Nest, they would have heard a large truck rumbling up the road.

Grandfather joined them then. "Ahhh. Thank heaven for hot coffee!"

"And hot chocolate!" said Benny.

True to his word, Grandfather had visited a store in Beaverton. He'd brought back chips, cookies, fruit, raisins, juices, and packets of cocoa.

The others entered the dining hall.

As always, Victor Lacey was in a cheerful mood. "Great morning for fishing!"

Mr. Williams only nodded curtly and sat away from the group.

When Marianne came in to pour their

coffee, Corey jumped up and asked if he could help.

"You're a guest," Marianne told him.

Looking downcast, Corey took his seat again.

Benny listened intently to the exchange. Was Marianne the whisperer outside their cabin the night before? Or was she the one with the shrill voice? It was hard to tell.

"I have an idea," announced Mr. Lacey. "Why don't you Aldens come fishing with me this morning?"

"I didn't bring my fishing gear," said Grandfather.

Mrs. Harrington came in to clear the bowls. "You can borrow my husband's rod. And the children can use the one a guest left behind. But don't expect much luck."

"I haven't caught a minnow since I've been here," Mr. Williams said. "I thought Tincup Creek was a gold-medal stream."

"What's that?" asked Jessie.

"It means it should be teeming with trout," Mr. Williams replied, heaving himself away from his meager breakfast.

Outside the dining hall two rods leaned against the log siding. Fishing tackle boxes — one new, one old — sat below.

Mr. Williams, who had walked out with them, took a bamboo rod and the beat-up tackle box. He stalked down the path alone.

"Don't you guys fish together?" Benny asked Victor.

The younger man shook his head. "Mr. Williams always fishes by himself."

Henry noticed Victor's metal rod and shiny tackle box. "That's a cool rod."

"Yeah, it's a beaut. The metal is titanium."

Henry also admired the wide belt around Victor's waist that carried pliers, a towel, and a holder for the rod. By comparison, Mr. Williams's old vest looked outdated.

The path divided at the banks of Tincup Creek. Mr. Williams went upstream. Victor led the Aldens downstream.

"Hope they're biting today," he said.

So did Benny. If they caught some fish, they'd have a good dinner that night.

First Victor showed them how to cast the

line into the water. "It's all in the wrist," he instructed.

Grandfather caught on quickly. So did Henry. Then Benny gave it a try. The children laughed when Benny's line got caught on a tree branch behind them!

Next they waded out into the creek. Mrs. Harrington had issued them all rubber boots. The water wasn't very deep, but it was chilly.

Victor splashed noisily through the stream, heading for a good sunny spot.

Way downstream, Henry could see Robert Williams wading slowly. The older man put each foot down quietly.

"This looks promising," Victor said, casting his line.

After everyone had cast a few times, Victor talked about the lures used in trout fishing.

"Trout will eat anything that looks like an insect," he said. His own vest displayed brightly colored feathered lures with hooks.

After about an hour, Henry caught a fish! Victor helped him reel in the baby brown trout.

"Way to go!" Victor praised, netting the fish.

Henry stared at the small fish struggling in the net. "It's too small. I want to turn him loose." He and Grandfather gently eased the hook from the trout's mouth and watched him swim away.

"There goes dinner!" Benny said mournfully.

"One little fish wouldn't feed all of us," Grandfather said. "I'm sure Mrs. Harrington will have a good supper tonight."

Jessie wasn't so sure. If the owner fixed a good supper, it would be the *first* time since they arrived.

Back on the bank, Victor packed up his gear. "Let's you and I talk business," he said to Grandfather.

"All right," Grandfather agreed.

"May we stay?" Jessie asked, pulling off her rubber boots. "We'd like to explore."

"Yes, but don't wander too far," said Grandfather.

The two men walked up the path toward Eagles Nest.

Leaving their boots, the kids strolled up-stream.

"There's Mr. Williams," Violet said.

The man stood stock-still in the shady shallows near a rocky outcropping. He cast expertly, his lead sinker plopping into the water with scarcely a ripple.

Benny waved, but Mr. Williams didn't look up. "Why is he so grouchy?" he asked.

"Fishermen are serious about their sport," Henry replied.

"He's grouchy when he's not fishing," Jessie pointed out.

"Maybe he's disappointed with Eagles Nest," suggested Violet. "The place hardly lives up to its claims."

As they walked farther upstream, the children were struck by the wild, unspoiled beauty of the land.

"I wish we knew why Mr. Lacey said Grandfather's property is worthless," Jessie said. "It's perfect."

Just then something hit Benny on the shin.

"Ouch!" he cried, hopping on one foot.

Violet examined his leg. "You've got a little scrape. It'll be okay. What did you bump into?"

They searched through the long grass and found a wooden stake. Tied to the stake was a taut length of white nylon cord. They followed the cord to the edge of the stream, where it disappeared underwater.

Kneeling on the wet stones, Henry tugged at the white cord. "There's a net on the end of this."

"A net?" Jessie questioned.

"Yeah, like a badminton net," Henry said. "It's tied on the other side, too."

Violet frowned. "Why would there be a net across the creek?"

"The net acts like a dam," Henry explained. "I bet it's holding back most of the trout. That's why Mr. Williams can't catch any fish. They're all trapped up here."

Jessie glanced downstream, thinking about Mr. Williams. At breakfast he had mentioned Tincup Creek was a gold-medal stream, yet Mrs. Harrington insisted the creek was all fished out. Why were the trout being penned way upstream?

Something was definitely fishy at Eagles Nest.

"What did Mr. Lacey want?" Henry asked Grandfather.

It was late afternoon. The children hadn't been able to speak to their grandfather until then. They were all sitting in the rockers on the dining hall porch.

James Alden paused before he spoke. "He offered double his original offer for my property."

"Why is he so anxious to buy your land?" asked Jessie.

"That's what I'd like to know," said Grandfather. "Why don't we visit our town again. Maybe the answer is there."

"We might see Rose's ghost!" Benny said, jumping up.

"Now, Benny," Grandfather said gently. "What have we said about ghosts?"

Deep inside, he knew Grandfather was right. But who was the mysterious Lady in Gray?

The Aldens went inside to ask to borrow Mrs. Harrington's Jeep.

"Going to Tincup again, eh?" she remarked, handing over the keys.

"I think we'll visit some buildings this time," said Grandfather. "Show the children a bit of history."

It was nearly sundown when they parked the Jeep and hiked down the wagon road into town.

Grandfather repeated his earlier warning. "Remember, these buildings may look okay, but be careful where you step."

They went into the dry goods store.

"Check this out!" said Henry, awestruck.

Barrels stood by the high, dusty counter. Behind the counter, shelves climbed to the ceiling. The shelves were empty, but Henry could imagine them stocked with canned food, bolts of fabric, tools, boots, and dozens of other items.

"It's spooky in here," Violet whispered. "I feel like I'm in the wrong time or something."

Jessie nodded. "Like people dressed in old-fashioned outfits will come in any second."

"That's the magic of old buildings," said Grandfather. "They let us experience a true sense of history."

As they headed back outside, Jessie cried, "Look! There she is!"

A figure glided ahead of them, toward the sinking sun. She wore the same gray dress and gray shawl.

"It's the ghost of Rose Payne!" Benny gasped.

"There aren't any ghosts!" Grandfather said. "Ma'am!" he called out. "Please stop! Ma'am!"

Everyone chased after the ghost.

But the woman rounded the corner of the last building in town, Anderson's Hotel. By the time the Aldens reached the corner, the street was empty.

"She's gone," said Henry. "Vanished."

"Nonsense," stated Grandfather. "People don't vanish."

"But ghosts do," said Benny.

CHAPTER 7

The Secret Cupboard

Everyone discussed the vanishing ghost at dinner that night.

"We saw Rose Payne," Benny insisted.

Grandfather said, "Benny, we've been over this. There are no ghosts."

"But we saw *some*one," Violet insisted. "We even followed her. But she vanished."

"Just like a ghost!" Corey leaned forward. He and Mr. Lacey were the only ones who had eaten the tough burgers that were supper that night. Jessie figured Corey cleaned his plate every meal because he didn't want to hurt Marianne's feelings. Both Marianne and Mrs. Harrington did the cooking at Eagles Nest.

"Or a real person who knows a hiding place," said Mr. Williams. He had come back from Tincup Creek without any fish and now sat discouraged over the awful hamburger and boiled cabbage supper.

"I'd like to see the ghost," Corey said.

"She only appears at sundown," said Mrs. Harrington.

"That's cool," said Corey. "Will you kids take me? Maybe we could have a picnic."

That sounded like fun to Benny. "May we go, Grandfather?" he asked eagerly.

"Corey is an experienced hiker," Grandfather acknowledged. "I think it would be all right."

"Yippee!" Benny said, forgetting the picnic would probably be as terrible as the other meals.

When supper was over, James Alden and Victor Lacey went for a walk to further discuss the property offer. Mr. Williams settled down with some fishing magazines in the sitting area.

Henry meant to tell the fisherman about the net stretched across the stream, but Corey was noisily scooping up the heavy white crockery dishes.

"Stop it," Marianne told him, annoyed.

"Make me," he teased. "I'm helping so you'll go for a walk with me."

Marianne's dark brows drew together. "I don't want to."

"Why? I'm cute, funny, likable." He grinned.

Marianne glanced meaningfully at the Alden children.

"Uh . . . we should go brush our teeth," Jessie said.

They left the dining hall.

"I don't want to brush my teeth," protested Benny.

Violet giggled. "We don't have to yet. But we should leave Marianne and Corey alone."

Instead of sitting in the rockers on the front porch, the children wandered around the back of the dining hall.

"Mrs. Harrington has put out the garbage already," Henry said, noting the sturdy, bear-proof cans lined up on the back deck.

"She probably has lots of it," Jessie said. "Nobody but Corey and Mr. Lacey ate that nasty meal. I don't know how they stand it."

"I don't know how Marianne and Mrs. Harrington stand their own cooking," Henry added. "If I were them, I'd hire a cook."

Benny was staring at the row of cans. Beside them was a white metal cupboard with a lock through the double handles. One door was open, the lock dangling loosely from its handle. Pretty fancy for a garbage container, he thought.

Suddenly he knew what was in the cupboard. Marianne and Mrs. Harrington *didn't* eat their own cooking.

"I bet I know what's in the cabinet," he declared.

"What?" asked Henry.

"Something good," said Benny. "Look, the door's open. Can I look inside?"

Jessie nodded. "I guess it's okay."

Benny ran up on the porch. "I knew it! Food! Pork and beans, fruit juice, cupcakes, pickles — "

Jessie suddenly felt nervous. "Come away from there, Benny. Mrs. Harrington might be back any minute."

"Maybe those things will be in our picnic tomorrow," Violet told him.

"Maybe." But he doubted it.

Jessie pointed to some wires leading to a hinged metal panel beside the door.

"That's the fuse box," she said. "Those wires are for the phone and electricity."

"I wonder why the phones and power are always going out," Henry said. "I wonder if Mrs. Harrington tries to make this place horrible on purpose."

"But why?" asked Violet. "She should *want* tourists to come, not scare them away."

"I think the key to this mystery," said Jessie, "is the Lady in Gray."

"We'll see her tomorrow," Violet said softly.

*   *   *

The next afternoon the children and Corey piled into the Jeep.

"Us old guys will stay behind and chew the fat," said Victor Lacey, waving them off.

"Chew the fat?" said Benny. "Is that what's in our picnic basket?" He wouldn't be surprised.

"I hope not!" Corey laughed, starting the Jeep with a roar. "Now you kids show me the way."

The road was as bumpy as ever. Jessie felt like her bones were being rattled.

Suddenly Corey hit a huge pothole and the Jeep halted.

"Uh-oh," he said, hopping out. He and Henry lifted the hood.

"Do you know anything about cars?" asked Henry.

"Oh, sure." Corey twisted knobs and pulled out oily dipsticks. After tinkering with the engine about fifteen minutes, he threw up his greasy hands. "She's a goner! We'll have to walk."

Violet hauled the picnic basket out of

the backseat while Jessie grabbed the plaid blanket Marianne had given them to sit on.

Jessie whispered to Henry, "I thought Corey could fix cars."

"That's what he said," he whispered back. "But all he did was check the oil and battery fluid."

When they reached the wagon trail leading down into the canyon, Corey took the picnic basket and blanket from the girls. *He's really nice*, Jessie thought. *If he weren't so loud, maybe Marianne would like him better.*

Corey was excited about everything in Tincup. He pretended to be a cowboy getting off his horse in front of the dry goods store, giving Benny a fit of giggles. After he looped imaginary reins over the hitching post, they went inside.

"Cool," Corey said. "I wish I lived in those days."

"Me, too," agreed Benny. He liked Corey.

Violet was checking the sky out the window. "The sun is starting to go down," she reported. "We'd better get ready."

But Rose never appeared. The sun faded over the rim of the canyon without any sign of the Lady in Gray.

"I guess even a ghost needs a night off," Corey joked.

Sitting on the blanket, they ate their supper — cheese and stale bread with boiled eggs.

"Don't you think the food here is lousy?" Jessie asked Corey.

He laughed. "If you had college food, you'd think this was great." He tipped his head back. "If I'm not mistaken, serious rain clouds are rolling in. We'd better hurry back."

They packed quickly. As they hurried down Main Street, Violet glanced back over her shoulder. She had a feeling someone was watching them.

Someone was!

Violet glimpsed half a shadowed face through the slatted swinging doors of the dance hall. A yellowed, gnarled hand gripped the edge of the door.

Was it the ghost of Rose Payne, scared off by

Corey's loud voice? she wondered. Afraid, Violet scurried to catch up with the others.

Without the Jeep, it was a long hike back to Eagles Nest. *Maybe I'm imagining things,* Violet thought. She decided not to tell anyone about the face.

Heavy clouds burst while the children were several yards from the motel. Soaked and shivering, they ran into the dining hall.

Grandfather had built a fire in the stone fireplace. Lanterns glowed on tables. The power was out again.

"The Jeep died," Corey explained, taking the thin towel Marianne handed him.

"So has the electricity and phones — *again*," said Mr. Williams with disgust. "I think I'll pack it in."

"You're leaving?" asked Mrs. Harrington. "In this storm?"

"It's not that far to Beaverton," said Mr. Williams. "At least I can get a decent meal! You can send me a refund in the mail." Then he stalked out of the hall, knocking over the stack of fishing magazines.

Henry and Benny bent to straighten the

pile. In the flickering lamplight, a picture caught Henry's eye. His suspicions about the two fishermen grew stronger.

"You guys get dry," Jessie told her brothers and sister. "I had the blanket over my head, so I'm not as wet as you are. I'll go to our cabins and bring dry socks and shirts."

"Take the umbrella." Grandfather handed her a black umbrella.

But when Jessie opened it outside, the umbrella was full of holes! Nothing worked at Eagles Nest!

"I'm better off without it," she muttered to herself.

As she skirted puddles, she saw Corey leaving his cabin. He wore a yellow plastic rain poncho and was heading for the dining hall.

Something peculiar was sticking out from under his poncho. It looked like the gray crocheted shawl worn by the ghost of Rose Payne!

Was Corey Browne pretending to be the ghost of Tincup?

CHAPTER 8

The Discovery

"This mystery keeps getting weirder and weirder," said Benny as he followed his brother up the steep path. "I wonder if that face you saw yesterday was Rose Payne." Violet had decided to share her sighting with her sister and brothers after all.

"I know," agreed Violet. She walked right behind Benny. "First there was that awful face, then Jessie saw the ghost's shawl under Corey's poncho. It really *is* weird."

It was a perfect day. Grandfather had

driven into Beaverton to meet with a real estate lawyer.

"I can't imagine why Mr. Lacey is offering me so much money," Grandfather had told the children after breakfast. "He keeps hounding me about selling the land. Maybe a real estate lawyer familiar with property around here can help me make a decision."

The children had looked at one another. They didn't want Grandfather to sell the land or the town. So after Grandfather drove away in the rental car, they decided to explore his property.

"Now, don't wander off," Mrs. Harrington warned them.

"We won't go far," Violet promised. "We want to hike and take some pictures."

Mrs. Harrington had frowned suspiciously, as if she didn't trust them.

Jessie carried the survey map. Benny and Henry toted small packs with their lunches, made from the groceries Grandfather had brought back from Beaverton the other day.

At the big rock, Jessie unfolded the map and studied it. "We know where Tincup is.

And we know which way Old Gert's cabin is. Let's go that way." She pointed east. "We haven't been in that direction yet."

Henry quickly located a trail and they began climbing. As they hiked, they went over the mystery.

"Mr. Williams is gone for good," said Henry. "We can scratch him off our suspect list."

"It looks like Corey is the ghost," said Jessie. "I mean, why else would he have that shawl?"

"But who did Violet see in the dance hall?" asked Henry. "It couldn't have been Corey. He was with us."

Violet shivered in the hot sun. "Oh! That was so scary! Her face was yellowed and wrinkled and her hands were like claws."

"She must be an old, old lady," Benny ventured. "Even older than Old Gert."

"But how could she live in that town?" Jessie asked. "Without food or running water or heat — . Hey, see what I found!" she exclaimed. She pointed to a pair of rusted metal rails. "Tiny train tracks."

"It's a tramway," said Henry, parting the weeds to examine the rails. "We must be near the silver mine."

"Oh, boy!" Benny cried. "Let's find the mine!"

"We have to watch out," Henry warned. "Old mine shafts are dangerous. You could walk right over it and fall in."

But the Tincup Silver Mine was easy to locate. All they had to do was follow the tramway tracks. At the end they found a ramshackle shelter that covered the mine entrance. The entrance had been boarded over, though some of the planks were rotted.

"Let's stay away from it," Jessie said. "The idea of a deep mine shaft makes me nervous."

"Time for lunch anyway," said Benny. At least today he'd have something good.

The kids found some square gray stones not too far from the mine. The sun-warmed stones made a perfect picnic table.

As she munched raisins, Violet stroked the hand-tooled granite. "You know what I think this is?" she said.

"What?" asked Jessie.

"What's left of Rose and Duncan Payne's mansion!"

Henry glanced around. "I bet you're right, Violet. These stones are the foundation. Over there is part of a wall. And those smooth flat stones are roofing slates."

She snapped a picture of the tumbled brick. "This was probably a beautiful place. It's a shame it's fallen down."

After lunch, the Aldens wandered around what was left of the Payne mansion. Benny found a teardrop-shaped piece of glass that sparkled in the sun.

"Oooh," he exclaimed. "Is this a diamond?"

"It's a crystal prism," said Jessie. "It's cut so it catches the light and throws rainbows. It probably came off a chandelier or a light fixture."

Benny held up the prism, letting the sun create rainbows. "Mrs. McGregor told me a story once, about a little boy who found a pot of gold at the end of a rainbow. I wonder if I can find one today!"

He scampered off, the prism dangling from his fingers.

"Benny, wait!" Jessie called.

Henry quickly gathered their lunch trash so they could follow him. "Why are we always running uphill?" he said, laughing as they caught up with their little brother.

Even Benny was tired. "I don't think I'll ever find the end of this rainbow!" He sank down on a log.

The others gratefully collapsed around him.

"I'm warm," Violet remarked.

"So am I," Henry said.

"No, I mean, I feel warm air." She put her arm out. "Stick your hand out there."

Henry put out his arm. "You're right. I do feel warm air. Where is it coming from?" He explored the stony outcropping and found a hole between two rocks. Warm air drifted from the hole.

"It's a cave," said Jessie, peering inside.

"I'm going in," Henry declared. "I have to find out about this air."

Violet was concerned. "Be careful, Henry."

"I will," he promised, wiggling his legs, then his body, through the hole.

The others gathered anxiously at the mouth of the cave.

"What do you see?" Benny called.

Silence.

Then Henry's voice echoed, "There are pools of water that are warm like baths! This is so neat!"

"Maybe you should come out now, Henry," said Jessie.

Seconds later, Henry's head and shoulders popped through the rocks. "You should see those steamy pools."

As they left the cave area to head home, the children discovered more small pools hidden among the rocks. The water was warm, as Henry had said. They took off their shoes and socks and soaked their feet.

"This feels great," Jessie said. "My feet were tired, but now I feel I could hike for ten miles!"

"Please," Henry protested. "Let's not! In fact, we should be getting back."

After putting their shoes and socks on

again, the children struck off down the mountain.

Suddenly they heard a crashing sound. Something was thrashing in the woods!

Jessie stared at Henry. "Is it a bear?" Bears lived in the Rockies.

They flew down the trail. This time even Benny was scared.

After they had run well past the thrashing noise, Henry stopped.

"What is it?" panted Violet.

"We're lost again. This is the trail to Old Gert's cabin," he said regretfully. "Sorry, guys."

Jessie said, "I don't think Old Gert is so bad. Mrs. Harrington makes her sound worse than she really is."

"She doesn't like anyone on her land," said Violet.

"We aren't moving in," said Jessie. "We're just asking for directions. The last time we stumbled on the trail home. But Gert must know a better way."

Benny was game. "Let's go see her!"

They reached the cabin shortly. This

time Benny strode up to the door and knocked.

The huge woman opened the door. When she saw Benny, she said, "What do you want? I thought I told you kids to keep off my land."

"We're lost again, Miss Gert," said Benny. "Can you tell us how to get to Eagles Nest? We don't want to see the ghost!"

"What ghost?" asked Old Gert, softening her tone slightly. Today she wore a blue plaid shirt over her jeans. Her belt was a piece of rope.

"The ghost of Tincup. Rose Payne," Violet explained. "We've seen her!"

The old woman snorted. "Is Adele Harrington still dragging out that old tall tale?"

"You mean there isn't any ghost?" asked Jessie. In her heart, she knew ghosts didn't exist, but the Lady in Gray was *so* mysterious. And they *had* seen her.

"You see," Henry added, "our grandfather owns Tincup and the land around it now."

"Is that right?" Gert seemed suddenly interested. "What's he planning to do with the land?"

"We don't know," Benny answered. "Another man wants to buy it from him. And he's not even scared of the ghost!"

Gert leaned against the doorway. "Let me tell you kids something. If you're so keen on the story of Rose and Duncan Payne, forget about the ghost."

"Forget about her?" repeated Violet.

"Yes," said Gert with emphasis. "Remember the descendants of Rose and Duncan. That might be the answer to your mystery."

"Who — " Jessie began, but the old woman pointed toward a grove of evergreens.

"Go through those trees," Gert directed. "The shortcut to Eagles Nest is on the other side."

Henry knew they had worn out their welcome. "Thanks very much," he said.

"One more thing," Gert called out to them.

The Aldens turned around.

"I've never met your grandfather, but please tell him for me that this land is home to many animals and birds." Her booming voice dropped. "And me. My land borders his. People should just . . . let us be."

"We'll tell him," Violet promised. Once again, she had that odd feeling about Old Gert. What *was* it?

As the children walked through the cool stand of trees, they talked about Gert's clue to the mystery.

"Who are the descendants of Rose and Duncan Payne?" Jessie asked, trying to recall the details of the story Mrs. Harrington told them the first night.

Violet knew. "They had one daughter. Her name was Seraphina. And Rose was supposed to be beautiful, with blue eyes and long black hair."

"Her daughter could have looked like her," said Henry. "And probably her children, if she had any."

The idea came to the kids at once.

"Marianne!" Violet cried. "She has blue eyes and long black hair. And she's really pretty. Is it possible she's related to Rose and Duncan Payne?"

Benny frowned. "Then wouldn't Mrs. Harrington be related to the ghost, too? She's Marianne's mother."

"Not necessarily," Henry said. "*Mr.* Harrington could be related to Seraphina. He married Mrs. Harrington, but she isn't related to the Paynes. But their child, Marianne, is."

"This is so confusing!" Jessie exclaimed. "Ghosts and mountain women and property . . . will we ever untangle this mixed-up mystery?"

"Gert seemed awfully worried about Grandfather selling the land to Victor Lacey," said Violet. "I wonder if she's afraid of Mr. Lacey making trouble for her."

"I can't imagine that lady being afraid of *anybody*," said Benny, making them laugh.

"The only way we'll solve this case," Jessie said, speaking for them all, "is to track down the ghost."

CHAPTER 9

The Ghost Hunt

The rest of the way back to the motel, the children figured out a plan. They would go alone into Tincup, just before sunset, and track down the Lady in Gray. This time she wouldn't get away.

"I'm nervous," Violet admitted. She couldn't forget the sight of the yellowed, wrinkled face she had seen leering through the slatted door.

"Me, too," Henry said. "The ghost is very lifelike. But we know it isn't real."

Jessie nodded in agreement. "We have to

catch her — or him. It's the only way to find out what's going on here. If Grandfather decides to sell the land to Victor Lacey, he could be making a big mistake. We have to do this for Grandfather."

"What will we do with the ghost when we catch it?" Benny asked, his eyes round. A ghost hunt sounded neat, but he was also frightened.

"It'll be okay," Violet reassured her little brother.

"We're the Aldens and we make a great team!" said Jessie, sounding like a cheerleader. "Let some old ghost try to get away from us!"

Benny giggled, feeling better.

At Eagles Nest, they found Grandfather and Mr. Lacey in deep conversation in the sitting area of the dining hall. Lunch was about to be served.

Grandfather waved them over. "Mr. Lacey and I have been talking about the land. I'm wondering if anyone will ever visit there. Or if we'll really use it. I'm thinking of selling it to Mr. Lacey."

Benny stared at Grandfather, his hunger forgotten. "You're going to sell the town? How can I be mayor and fire chief and police chief?"

"Oh, Benny," Mr. Lacey said enticingly. "You don't want to be in charge of a run-down old town."

"Lunch!" Mrs. Harrington called to the guests.

Jessie was amazed to see Corey Browne carry a huge bowl of soup from the kitchen. Marianne followed him with a large basket of bread. He looked at her as he set down the bowl, spilling the soup a little. Jessie could tell Corey was head over heels for Marianne Harrington. And for once, she wasn't acting like she couldn't stand him. Did Corey finally win her over?

Jessi dipped her spoon into her soup. Yuck. It was like dishwater with a few soggy carrots floating around. She broke off a hunk of stale bread to dunk in the thin soup. Like Benny, she was tired of the awful food.

"Excellent soup!" Victor praised Mrs.

Harrington, scraping his bowl. "I'll have seconds, if you have enough."

"Oh, there's plenty," said Mrs. Harrington. "By the way, dinner will be late tonight. The power is off again."

Violet noticed a mysterious glance pass between Victor Lacey and the owner as she ladled more watery soup into his bowl. Something strange was going on, but she didn't have time to think about it now.

"Grandfather," she announced. "Is it okay if we go down to Tincup? We know the way. And it's not that far to walk. We've gotten pretty used to hiking."

"We'll be careful," added Henry. "We won't go into any of the buildings. We just want to walk through the town."

He crossed his fingers under the table. This was an important part of their plan. Everyone in Eagles Nest had to know they were going to Tincup. And Grandfather had to give his permission.

"Well . . ." James Alden hesitated. "You are responsible children. I trust you. If you leave early and promise to be back well before dark, it'll be fine."

"We will," said Benny. The first part of their plan had worked!

The children prepared for the hike immediately after lunch. Jessie packed snacks and bottles of water that Grandfather had brought back from his second trip to Beaverton.

"We can eat on the way," she told the others. "That soup wouldn't give a chipmunk strength."

As they walked behind the dining hall, they noticed the gray metal panel was hanging open.

"The fuse box!" exclaimed Henry. He looked inside. Sure enough, one of the fuses was missing. "I bet that goes to the electricity."

"Now we know Mrs. Harrington turns off the phones and power on purpose," said Benny.

"We'd better hurry," Violet said. "We don't have the Jeep to ride in and we must be in Tincup by sunset."

Although that seemed like a lot of time, lunch had been late and they had to pack for the hike. It was after two-thirty when the Aldens set off on the potholed road.

The day was clear but very warm. Before they had walked far, the children were glad Jessie had told them to put on short-sleeved T-shirts and shorts. Stout walking shoes prevented twisted ankles and sore feet.

Soon they were panting as they climbed the steep mountain.

"I wish we had the Jeep," Jessie said. "It was bouncy, but it got us to the trail a lot quicker!"

"I like walking," Benny said. As always, he had the most energy. "You can see the plants and birds this way."

Jessie checked her watch. Almost three-thirty. They had been walking for nearly an hour and they hadn't reached the end of the road yet. She had forgotten how long the road was.

Suddenly Violet stumbled and cracked her knee on a rock.

"It's nothing," she told Henry, who gently felt the swelling.

"You might get a bruise," he said. "Maybe we should stop. Walking on it could make it worse."

"I'm okay," Violet insisted. Her knee hurt only a little. She couldn't let the others and Grandfather down.

"Are you sure?" asked Jessie, concerned. Of them all, Violet tended to be the most quiet.

Violet smiled gamely. "Positive."

The children slowed their pace so Violet could keep up. It was after five when they reached the end of the potholed road.

"Here's the old wagon trail," Benny said.

It took them another thirty minutes to walk down the twisting road. By now, Violet's knee had stopped hurting, but they still took it easy.

When they reached Tincup, the children stared at one another. As bravely as they had talked on the hike, their fears were back.

"We're all scared," Jessie said. "But this

is for Grandfather. If he doesn't know the truth, he could be making a mistake. And we owe it to Gert to save the land."

"Jessie's right," said Violet. She drew in a deep breath. "The sun is nearly over the canyon. Let's go catch the ghost."

"It's not a real ghost," Henry said firmly. But he was as nervous as the others. Saying there were no ghosts and *seeing* one were two different things.

Together, the Aldens entered the silent ghost town. The wind had risen again, kicking tumbleweeds ahead of them. A loose shingle shrieked.

They decided to wait for full sunset by the dance hall, where Violet had seen the old crone's face.

The sun dropped in a lazy arc till it touched the craggy ledge of the canyon.

And then they saw her.

She appeared from nowhere, gliding into the dusty street in her tattered gray dress, the gray shawl draped about her shoulders.

The Aldens stood rooted for a few seconds. Then Henry shouted, "Okay, guys. Let's move!"

They ran then, with Jessie in the lead.

Jessie stared at the figure ahead of her. The Lady in Gray didn't speed up or act as if she heard pounding feet behind her.

But Jessie didn't see any shoes sticking out from under the hem of the gray dress. *Was* this Rose Payne, walking toward the sunset to meet her husband as she'd done for so many years? But she couldn't let such thoughts take over. She had to catch this ghost.

Sprinting, Jessie pulled away from the others. She was beside the Lady in Gray now. The figure turned her face sharply away from Jessie.

Swallowing her fear, Jessie grabbed one thin arm and yanked the figure around.

Amazed, she gasped at the yellowed, wrinkled face surrounded by wisps of scraggly gray hair. The yellowed hand Jessie grasped felt horrible, but she didn't let go.

Instead she reached up and pulled off the gray wig. The yellowed crone mask came off with it.

She found herself staring into the startled blue eyes of Marianne Harrington.

"You!" Jessie accused. "You're the ghost!"

The others ran up.

"It's Marianne!" Violet said. "She's the Lady in Gray!"

Pulling off the fake rubber hands, Marianne began to cry.

At that moment, Victor Lacey blasted through the rickety swinging doors of the dance hall.

"All right, you kids!" he said menacingly. "I knew you were trouble the minute I laid eyes on you. Now I'll have to fix you but good!"

Before the children had a chance to be frightened by his threat, a second voice boomed from the dry goods store.

"You'll do nothing of the sort, you little weasel!"

Benny hopped up and down. "It's Gert!"

It was indeed Old Gert. She loomed in

the center of the road, her booted feet spread wide apart. No one was going anywhere without dealing with her.

"You leave these children alone," she told Victor. "The jig is up. I'm on to your little game."

"So are we," said Henry. "But we needed to bring the 'ghost' out in the open first."

Suddenly Violet figured out the missing piece that had been bothering her. They were on the wrong track! Marianne Harrington wasn't the descendant of Rose and Duncan Payne.

Old Gert was!

CHAPTER 10

Benny's Gift

Violet drew in a breath. It all fit. Old Gert had the brightest blue eyes Violet had ever seen. And Gert's iron-gray hair had probably once been long and black.

"You're related to Rose and Duncan," she said to Gert.

The blue eyes twinkled. "I wondered when you'd guess! Yes, I'm Seraphina's granddaughter. I was born back East, where Seraphina married. My father, her son, also stayed in the East. But when we visited out here, I knew where I belonged. I came out here as soon as I finished school."

At that moment, a roaring sound made them all turn toward the top of the old wagon road above. The Jeep, which Marianne had had fixed, screeched to a stop. Grandfather, Corey Browne, and Mrs. Harrington hopped out. They wasted no time hiking down the wagon road into Tincup.

Grandfather strode over to the children. "Are you okay? I was worried when you didn't come back for supper."

"Grandfather!" Benny exclaimed. "You can't sell our town! We know the truth!"

"They don't know anything!" Victor Lacey blurted. "Who'd listen to a bunch of kids, anyway?"

"I would." James Alden crossed his arms over his chest.

Marianne Harrington was still crying. She sobbed on Corey's shoulder.

Victor threw her a disgusted look. "Oh, for Pete's sake, stop sniveling! If you hadn't messed things up, we could have pulled it off."

"I think you've bullied enough people," said Old Gert. "Why don't you come clean, Lacey."

But Victor wasn't about to confess that easily. "Those kids are so smart — let *them* tell what they think I've done."

"Go ahead," James Alden encouraged his grandchildren.

Henry began, "From the beginning, things didn't add up. First, Eagles Nest isn't what it claims to be."

"I do my best," said Mrs. Harrington.

"You try to drive people away," Henry told her. "You deliberately made the food awful and pulled the fuse that works the electricity. You unplugged the phone wires, too."

"That's not true!" Mrs. Harrington argued.

"It is true," Grandfather said, backing up Henry. "I've never stayed in a place with such lousy service. Even Mr. Williams left."

"That's because he was a real fisherman," Benny said, taking up the story. "Henry and I saw pictures in a magazine showing the way fishermen dress. Mr. Lacey's stuff is too new. Like he's never used it."

"Not only that, but the trout are trapped upstream with a net that goes all the way across Tincup Creek," Henry added. "We found the underwater net. No wonder it's so hard to catch any fish."

"So what does that prove?" Victor challenged.

Now Violet spoke up. "Nothing, by itself. But there are more pieces to the puzzle."

"Why would I drive off customers?" asked Adele Harrington. "Eagles Nest is how I earn my living."

"The motel isn't what it used to be," said Jessie. "But if you had a bigger place, like a fancy hotel, and a lot of land, more people would come up here."

Victor snorted. "People would need more than a bigger hotel to come here."

"What about warm springs?" Henry said. Victor paled visibly. "We found the springs this morning, the bubbling water in the cave and the creeks around it."

Now Old Gert turned to him in surprise. "The healing springs! I remember stories about the Ute Indians who came here to soak in the baths. But we thought it was only a legend. Not even the miners ever stumbled on the springs."

Grandfather smiled. "If there is a secret, leave it to my grandchildren to find it! I think I know where this is leading. The springs are on my land. And you want my property desperately. Why, Lacey?"

Now Victor sighed in resignation. "I'm into land development. But my last deal was a huge flop. I needed a better project, one that would make tons of money for me and my investors."

"And pay off your debts," Mrs. Harrington said acidly. "He made me all kinds of promises. I would be the manager of his fancy hotel. I'd have a whole staff to order around instead of cooking and cleaning rooms myself."

Victor ignored her bitter comments. "This was the perfect place to build a resort. Unspoiled, untouched. Course, we'd have to put in a real road and tear down this eyesore of a town — "

"Our town!" Benny exclaimed in protest.

"The springs would draw people here," Victor went on. "Many people who have pain believe in the healing powers of warm mineral baths. I'd planned to open the cave and put a fancy spa over the springs. Hot tubs, attendants to give massages. The guests would be totally pampered."

"What about the wildlife?" Gert asked. "Where were they supposed to go? And me?"

Victor waved his hand dismissively. "There are other mountains."

Grandfather turned to Adele Harrington. "How did you join Lacey's scheme?"

"He stayed at Eagles Nest." Mrs. Harrington shrugged. "I saw his blueprints one evening and we got to talking. I fell for his dream, hook, line, and sinker."

"You were going to sell him Eagles Nest, weren't you?" Henry guessed. "And you both knew that Grandfather owned the land where Tincup and the springs are."

"Yes," confessed Mrs. Harrington. "Victor wanted as much property as possible to make this a first-class resort. He was going to have a stable of horses, a ski lodge, hiking trails, the spa, and of course Tincup Creek, which *is* a gold-medal stream. It was his idea to dam up the trout so no one would catch any fish and leave."

"How did you know I'd come here with my grandchildren?" James Alden asked Victor. "I came out once to sign the papers when I bought the land from Jay Murphy."

Victor gave a nasty smile. "I was in the courthouse in Beaverton that day. I'd found the springs by accident and was looking in deed books to see who owned the property. Turns out a man named James Alden had just purchased the very land I needed. I overheard you talking to the clerk, saying you wanted to show the land to your grandchildren. That's when Mrs. Harrington and I put our heads together. We knew you'd have to stay at Eagles Nest. When you got here, we'd be ready."

"Poor food and no electricity at a motel would hardly force me to sell my property," Grandfather said.

"True," Victor agreed. "But if we made

you uncomfortable, you might fall for the important part of our scheme."

"The ghost," Jessie stated.

"Yes, the ghost of Tincup." Victor sounded almost proud. "The story is true, by the way. We just needed to bring the Lady in Gray to life, so to speak."

"You got Marianne to play the role," said Violet. "She and her mother were the only two who fit the part. Gert was too big — "

"As if I'd ever go along with such foolishness!" Gert sputtered.

" — and Mrs. Harrington was busy running Eagles Nest," Violet said. "So that left Marianne."

Realizing it was her turn to speak, Marianne sniffed and said, "I never liked the idea of pretending to be the ghost. Especially after I met you Aldens. You're such nice people. But my mother always dreamed of owning a fine hotel and Victor offered her that chance. I couldn't stand in her way."

"But you quit, didn't you?" asked Benny. "We heard you arguing outside our window with your mother."

"Yes," Marianne said. "I really hated wearing that ridiculous outfit to fool Mr. Alden so he'd sell his land. One night I told my mother I wouldn't do it anymore."

Now Jessie broke in. "Corey almost took over for you. I saw him with part of the costume under his poncho the evening of the rainstorm."

Corey looked sheepish. "Victor Lacey came to me. He knew I'd do anything for Marianne, so I offered to dress up as Rose Payne. I'm in the Drama Club at school."

Victor looked angry. "I was in a real bind without our leading player. But Corey couldn't have pulled it off. He's too big. You people would know in an instant he wasn't the ghost of a woman. But he was easily roped into my plans."

"You rigged the Jeep so it broke down when we went to Tincup that evening," said Henry. "You said you knew how to fix cars but you didn't do anything. We walked into Tincup to give Marianne time to get into her costume."

Corey nodded. "There's another path you Aldens don't know about. We decided, instead of the ghost 'walking' again, to have Marianne hide behind the dance hall door. One of you was bound to see her."

"I did." Violet shuddered at the memory of that horrible face.

"I'm sorry," Marianne apologized. "But in the end I couldn't be disloyal to my mother. She's worked so hard all these years and there was a chance for her to make it."

Victor smacked his fist into his open palm. "If you Aldens hadn't come along, I'd be on my way to becoming a very rich man. Mr. Alden was ready to sell me his property — "

Grandfather held up a hand. "Not so fast. I wasn't sure what your game was. My grandchildren uncovered it."

"Does this mean you're not selling our town?" asked Benny.

Grandfather smiled at him. "Tincup is ours. And all the property around it." He looked at Old Gert. "I'm aware that your land is next to mine."

She looked worried for the first time. "I've always lived there."

"And you will continue to live there," Grandfather assured her. "I'm not touching the property. I do think the town of Tincup ought to be saved, though. It's part of history. I plan to pave the road and have the buildings preserved. People would love to tour an old silver-mining town."

Marianne turned excitedly to her mother. "We'll have real tourists, Mother. And they'll need a place to stay!"

"Well, it won't be at Eagles Nest," said Mrs. Harrington. "I'm selling. To Mr. Alden, if he wants it. I'm tired of running a motel in the middle of nowhere. It's time for us to move on, Marianne. Make a new start."

"You can always go to Colorado State," Corey said. "It's a good school and the town is nice, too."

While they were talking, Henry noticed Victor Lacey slipping between two of the buildings.

"Hey!" he cried. "Mr. Lacey is trying to get away!"

The children dashed down the alley. Corey and Old Gert, who could run surprisingly fast, reached the man first.

"My dream is up in smoke," Victor declared. "I'm leaving!"

"But you've caused people a lot of trouble," said Grandfather. "You can't just walk away like nothing has happened. Gert, what do you think we should do?"

Gert thought a few seconds. "You know what would be a fair punishment? Victor ought to camp in Tincup overnight. The bears *might* not smell him."

"Bears?" Victor said shakily. "You're going to leave me alone here with bears around?"

Corey went up to the Jeep and brought down a blanket, a bottle of water, and a bag of trail mix.

Gert stood guard at the entrance to the town. "Don't worry, Mr. Alden. I'll make sure our 'pampered guest' doesn't leave before daybreak."

As the others climbed the trail out of Tincup, Benny asked, "Are there bears?"

"Only in the wilderness areas," Grandfather answered. "They are shy and would rather not be around people."

Benny turned back. Victor Lacey wore the blanket over his shoulders and a glower on his face.

"Sweet dreams!" Benny said.

The next morning, Mrs. Harrington and Marianne prepared a real rancher's-style breakfast with the eggs, bacon, biscuits, and butter they had been hoarding in the secret cupboard.

The children ate until they were stuffed.

As Grandfather was sipping a second cup of coffee, a knock sounded at the dining hall door.

It was Gert, with Victor in tow. Victor Lacey straggled behind her, contrite and bedraggled. Jessie figured he hadn't slept much.

"Have some breakfast," Adele Harrington offered them.

"Don't mind if I do," said Gert, sitting down.

But Victor shook his head. "No, thanks. I'll just pack and be on my way." He hurried out of the dining hall.

Moments later, they heard his rental car engine start and roar down the road.

"We'll be leaving tomorrow ourselves," said James Alden. "I'll be in touch about buying Eagles Nest."

"Marianne and I will fix a nice supper tonight," said Mrs. Harrington gratefully.

Gert reached into her pocket. "I have something for you, Benny. It's from the old Tincup Mine."

Benny stared in amazement at the worn silver coin she dropped into his hand. "A real coin! Gee, thanks."

"Keep it to remind you of this trip," Gert told him. "And I'll see you when you come back."

Violet knew they would be back, to see Tincup restored to its former glory.

Meanwhile, she bet there were other adventures right around the corner.

GERTRUDE CHANDLER WARNER discovered when she was teaching that many readers who like an exciting story could find no books that were both easy and fun to read. She decided to try to meet this need, and her first book, *The Boxcar Children*, quickly proved she had succeeded.

Miss Warner drew on her own experiences to write the mystery. As a child she spent hours watching trains go by on the tracks opposite her family home. She often dreamed about what it would be like to set up housekeeping in a caboose or freight car — the situation the Alden children find themselves in.

When Miss Warner received requests for more adventures involving Henry, Jessie, Violet, and Benny Alden, she began additional stories. In each, she chose a special setting and introduced unusual or eccentric characters who liked the unpredictable.

While the mystery element is central to each of Miss Warner's books, she never thought of them as strictly juvenile mysteries. She liked to stress the Aldens' independence and resourcefulness and their solid New England devotion to using up and making do. The Aldens go about most of their adventures with as little adult supervision as possible — something else that delights young readers.

Miss Warner lived in Putnam, Connecticut, until her death in 1979. During her lifetime, she received hundreds of letters from girls and boys telling her how much they liked her books.